How Dell, Apple, HDMI, BenQ, HP, Levono, Google, Yahoo, Microsoft, Firefox Function in my dreams when I land on Moon!

Martha Minow
Heidi Cruz
Peter Sherwood
Pamela Murphy
Mimi Schapiro
Susan Dell
Melinda Gates
Sandy West
Paula Clancy
Mary Fisher
Judy Wang
Patricia Gay
Uwe Gordon
Kora-Leah Meet Faust Wilson
Sherry Kim
Barbara Bush
Aime Wood
Kathleen Stephan
Jennifer Sharp
Janet Boggs
Susan Wojcincki
Alison Schmidt
Ashley Biden
Ann Jobs
Tyrek Knapp
Bob Yong
Steven Pence
Kristen Yan
James Galway
Kristen Bezos

Whitney Bank
CARD service
Aly Buffett
Skylar Zhang
Laura Brown
p. o. Box 40195
Gulfport, MS 39502

Tulsa Ally Bank
Tom L. Wu
Eric Wood
Patti Johnson
1400 Webster Street
New Orleans, LA 70125

ReMax, Lakeside
Megan Barry
Kai Trump
Spencer Kushner
Sheng Wu
Yosemite Jackson
Karen Batten
Donald Trump
27169 HWY 189 Suite 1
Bush, CA 92317

Abbey Fittstown, McKenna Euphrosine at Epcot, Orlando, FL

Nelson-wilson construction, inc.
Yiwan-hjeekim art memory,
A mimi-brain technology
Rises on facebook of J. Gray Camp,
Why Stephan Lewandowsky pick Amelia Jay / Murphy Fan?

Tom and Katie disagree?
Hanks and Banks fight a war?
Brad and Angie not knowing Sasha Obama?
Christy Morrissey and Mark Brown not giving up?

Kun Zhao,
Yao Yao,
Changxing Miao,
Quanshen Jiu,

Pigong Han,
Bolin Guo,
Ping zhang,
Qingbo Dong,

Daihong Zhu,
Wangbing Dai,
Wenhui Wu,
Do they know Bona-Constantin a lot?

Arts and Soul Outlooks

Infirmary Band
George Peabody
Thomas Boyd,
Mike Donahue
Dalrymple Tower
Murphy j. Roster
Ruffin Pleasant
Taddy Porter
Carta Blanca
Dos Equis
Scotch Whisky
Jimmie Lawson
Xiaoliang Wan
JIuyi Zhu
Fang Wang
Amber Law
Rebecca Docter
MinH Kiet
Josh Jackson
Heng Yang
Chang Sha
Wu Han
John Weinman
John Nicklow
Josepg Butt
James Edgar Monroe
Gregory Choppin
Dmitri Mendelevium

Flying kites? With who? A wonder by Aber Naturlich

There, a kite,
Here, a boy,

Mark jannot smiles
Sam firefox reads William skiles

Left, keith leftwich
Right, david yarnold,

High up, janet ruscher
Low down, nicholas mayer

Written, david roux
Post up, Sharon Richardson

Coughing crow, hanah bienen,
Laughing parrot, Emily farris,

Constance, webster
Anniciation, patton

Aris Kobertis' Wonders over Onkle Gerald

He is distant
Refusing to show up at google

But, a friend from rome
Comes to conculusions
High technology has more
Than one locations:
Frankford, Florence, Brandon,
Mykonos, Patmos, Santonini,
London, Mountain View, Daly City,
…
Anthem is flying away
From Rome

Judith Page's Gossney Marywood observation

Anil Kashyap in Murphy institute
Nunemaker Auditorium,
Loyola University Thomas Hall,

Faces of Maya,
Tulane University Dinwindie Hall,

Woldenburg Art Center,
Kunshan Duke University
Ted Cruz, Kim Nelson, Michael Fitts, Gina Noble, Mary Fallin, Tiffany Chase

Jorie Graham as 2017 Florie Gale Arons poet
Kendall Cram, a reformer on Taylor Newday by Justin Massa
Richard Allen in West Virginia technology

Invisible hands
Notable and portable
We type, typos, despite the Thunder Storm wind

Ksenija Madzarevic

She is here
Typing
She is gone
Hiding

She plays pingpong
Skill hiking
She dives 3-m board
Deep=rooted civilian

David Armentor, Radboud University, Nijmegen....

Where he is at?
Why he trusts San Francisco?
When does he graduate?
How can he be so deceiving?

David armentor
Stephanie clough
Christy Crosby
Richard powell…

David armentor visits oxford
Making friends with umar manzoor
When pert linden hovius joins,
All three laughing…

Louisiana State University plus the Daily Reveille

Rolling stones
Raining frogs
The earth is horrified by odds and dots
The floor is filled with trunkful twigs

I eye scan
Knowing the unknowing
Who is watching me?
If you disagree to understand, then quit connecting

Names landfill

Carlsberg
Chimes
Gator
Keri Jackson
Josefin Dolsten
Barbara Robinson Picou

Samuel Adams
Juan Celaya-Hermandez
JBriann Johnson
Skylar Zhang
Christina Li
David Lee
Eric Wu
Guoliang Hu
Zhixiong Fu
Biyun Fu
Yongtao Yan
Zhiyuan Yang
Yongcui Yan
Pengchuan Yan
Qingbo Yan
Rongji Zhu
Mingying He
Hongjun Han
Ping Li
Xiaoyan Tan
Zhiwen Wang
Yongqi Liang
Juji Gu
Xiaodong xie
Zhongbing Zhang
Mackenzie bezos
Li Ping

Arthur Frescott
Oscar Allen
Kathy Ullkins
Sarah Robert
Bobby Jindal
F. King Alexander
Sharon Weston Broome
Lynne Bunch
Jacob Maranto
Yiduo Wen
Deyi Diao

Cui Er zhao
Zhaoming peng
Zhaokun peng
Zhaojun peng
Yan Jun
Yan Jung
Vitter .
Victor Page
Morris K.
Mac Hyman
David Yang
Huarong qu
Qing yan
Furong deng
Ying liu
Ji yan
Stephanie weeks
Melissa brackley
Caiping peng
Cai e peng
Mei e peng
Qingming peng
 Li guan
Yongshun yan

Uppsala university with Kathy ulkins

Ja'Vente smart on Wangyu
Kaylee Poche on Deng Ying
Christina David on David Boyd
Mackenzie Treadwell on Qu huarong
Abbie Shull of m. c. chang
Hailey Auglair of shuiling liu
William taylor potter on curt sharp
Kennedi landry on chenxi wu

Connor culp on ryan has
Isabella allen on yan liu
Clarke perkins on jiuyi zhu
Ethan gilbert on chuanzhen peng
Ramsina odisho on yuewan peng
Evan sacks on venessa Jefferson
Michael fits on caroline cruz
John nicklow on matthew Schapiro
Morton Schapiro on Sophia bollag
Eric Schmidt on beth bailar
Chuck robins on ryan haas
John chamber on Sabrina Ku
William mayer on meet bogue
Jerry brown on aly buffett
Ann hargis on lily milwit
Melania trump on samba beredjicek
Sam Walton on lucas wood
David murphy on mariet nguyen
David boren on jeff bezos
William bus jaco on sophiedun xu

For leigh Flexner –a quote from j. poggi, sarah abbott

Lenvy says more than
He does, rule of thumb,
One who serves, with or
Without doubt, rain or
Shine, we swim in a
Freedom pool, putting some
Worry-free mood in our skin
Life is better

When all bear some differences

Chimes, fishbone, dante's café

Wang yu
Jing yu,
Shan yu,
Li yu

Yao yao
Peng yao
Qiong Yao,
Ming yao

Jizhong zhang, ping ni,

Chun ni, jingping peng,
Good fish, well done Aligators
Brown and Samuel
All poetic masters

Here, beth beilar sings Winn V Dixie,
Barbara LeBlanc signs Walmart
Sula Kim adds Sam Walton to Tulane
Jesmyn Ward and Kenneth Ward make friends with Ruth Porat,

An art from scholastic , Li Chang, Yong Cheng, Yingping Peng, Zaiya Galway

Alan noel
He s a tough guy
Wondering why
His papers are left out

Giant science
Boris Kulikov paints human airbus
Kathleen krull writes about Leonardo and vinci

Grape Pritchard roads

Versailles Panama Crossways
New adams Edeneve styles
Orleans state parks

Feast on poems along st. Augustine street

I hear
Paul Allen
He peeks at my computer screen
A patient Man

My figures shake
Feel the urge to scream
I block my ears
Not knowing Bill Gates and Pheobe and Rory Gates near

My foot moves about

strangers mumble
Jennifer and Angelina argue
All about who shall go beyond Julia Roberts,

Birnam, Latter, Clancy, Hendrickson, fisher, Baples, blair, young, bezos
Nix, anon, jiasaw, bush, Clinton, Obama, Honolulu, trump, seattle,
The universe is masked by decorations
This is why Patrick Walsh and Scott Pippen rock

Vitter, Victor, Huy, Choy, Amelia, Donna, Hannah, Cora, Frances, Julie….

Dcoy in Erin Ganaway
The heat withdraws
A misfire burns
Smoking a bur tomato soup
A jarred ladybug
Jigging a lure across redbud river
I put a wooden duck in a pond
Trusting the wisdom of Jerry, Tom, Gerald, Vickii, Dulane, G. T., Robin, Akiko, Yuri,
The day grows grey
Under autumn season
The T N T lawn mower decides to rest at Australia,
We jump over piles of leafy lawn

Knowing a winter awaiting
Who else worrying?
Susan? Peter? James? Larry?
Li Zhang stopped crying,
So does Susan Haydon Bourne
I do admire Steven and his way to driving to Dallas, to Helena, and to Lawrence,
I wish that Mark Wrighton can invite him in
Give Jonathan/ Sheryl Zanhogs some oinky pin in their shy chins

Alan Fox, Tim Green, David Navas' Rypa Graphics

Huge green evergreens
Contrasting cold wind blows
Dots of brown-orange leaves
They Bob Young a 7-year old girl's wonder
Ben Franklin recall john Adams,
Writing a Rattle-Young-Poets-Jinglayebim anthology
A note on Lauriel –MARK—gONzles
Amit Ghosh and Sundar Pichai behave nice
Milton-Sherman, Howard-Earhart all fall silent

So, shea Dobson, paul haney adopts Shelby nathanson and john allen taylor

A redivider staff rooster
Crowing a middle-aged story by Emerson college
How well Olivia Woods feel?
Why does Molly Williams cry?
Charlotte Seley sits anxiously,
Dream hooding new Orleans under Jordan Escobar

Jack ma have gone to Africa
Ran Wang decides to join Frankford air force
We watch
Praying,
Hope that shawn, Trevor, Kaci, Tonya, Jason, Cox, Amanda, Sue, Jordan stay well

Wise owl feathers on café hirt Gaysteins

Silly frogs
They hide on lily pads
Croaking about empty sky

Rice paddles
A young plant is named Adrian Castro
Which sets Gabi desert as Fairland

French ada elen vio
Ialian pizza rosaoctivia

A dog Joliet Costco in my neighbor's home

I will travel
Along with Huaiying river
Snapshotting south America map
In eyes of Vincent Cellucci
And ear of Christopher Shipman
Lafayette, LA
Baton Rouge, LA
Metairie, LA,
Bo and Meow run fast,
Judging Miebrayson a lot,
Of course, only by mistakes

A dozen ordinary seniors of 2017, from new Orleans, come to my view

A few names,
They crawl hard,
Through hotwired doors
Into somewhere,
Flashing

Kathryn fasold, todd bacile,
Stephnie mayer, morgan faust,
Anne carr, jim lockwood,
Kaylie nguyen, jim guffgan,
Jenna Thomas, matt lemmler,
Maeve storm, josh danzig,
John parish, gay patricia,
Cherie Gauthier, abbie shull,
Melinda Richard, Kaylee poche,
Jan tankersley, bobby crane,

Christine harper, robin roche,
Stacey dinnell, karon George
Michelle herrandez, Nathaniel Jackson
Lavone tyree George, greater Andrew, samrufz hillford
Tyler myrick, michelle kendrickson
Michelle nuylan, tania estacion,
Jordan wood, carlos Valerio-kelly,
Jefferson parish, sarah parish,
Vone George, Edwin cruz,
Earhart college, Valerio yenny,
Amber marie Shinault, yan ji, wu jiahong, tom l. wu, sheng wu
4803 zenith street, Apt. b.
Metarie, LA 70001
Peng hounian and yan simei
1423 Webster street
New Orleans, LA 70015

Bier-stube has dieter, Arlen, Nicolson, s. Genois, and Calliope in

At the corner of bloomingdale and earhart
I see st. alan and st. sarah smiling
A fancy is set
Cornerstone of Cambridge
Martha and Joseph, Norman and Josephine, mira and john,
Palmetto, Abilene, Augusta, Aiqin, Chongqing, Qing huang dao, Yan An, jing Gang
shan, shan xi, shaanxi, wuhan , wuxi, wuhu, hangyang, Taiyuan, Fushun, Xiangfan,
Xiangyang, Changsha, Guiyang, jilin, Changchun, Yinchuan, Guangzhou, sanya, xi'an

Texas is my dream
Ohio is my hometown
Florida is my friend,
New mexico is a place I go during Christmas,
Iowa is a summer time treatment
New York State GIVES ME WINGS TO FLY
Louisiana is my vacation destination

Gregory choppin, wiin v Dixie, alan Yulman,
Xavier university, → ^^ Dixon

Mary and William McCarthy ballroom
A huge treetop near Cliojay hall
Sleetrump and robin Barton win Lottery , often

Alan Yu,
She remembers Tang Gangqing, Zhu Qun E, and Kathryn Drexel
Nick Murphy
He adds Microsoft to his Harbin computer screen

" the culture overall is spend now, worry later"

-----Matthew Wu

"they will go broke before they miss out on what they perceive to be a good opportunity to have fun their classmates."

Tayla Moore via Asher Baden in tulane Hullabaloo quotes section

Two haiku writers: Haxton and Richardson

One is Elaine Parker Adams,
Another is Shana Renee burris,
The bear is called Bailey Obama
The lotus flower blooms Mediasla Trumptown

Julia Feherbrene and susan Boggs do poetry
Jingle Yan and Thomas Owen Washington do stories
All write full screen dramas
Making half of the Arctic ocean run dry

Walmsley I><J   Trianon plaza

Satsuma, Gregonne,
Persimmon, Argonne,
Broadway to new York
Niagara to Pine
Forshey to Yeoman
Ramjeegina to Audubonsray

Colapissa / Monroe
Julioet /Olean
Fig / Miatletoe Street
St. Augustine high School

Hohoho, Santa Clause is Who Shu Moe???!!!!

Harvey square and Covington city
Jake hargis, Christine fallin,
Trenton Loyola, lost bayou,
Jimmy Brossard, Metairie lamb,
Rob taylor, bremier Nissan, todd bacile,
Alphabet pre-school, morgan faust,
Kun zhao, li guan,
Yiyang she, tien le,
Jung yan, chuanxian peng,
Aaa+ ramada inn,, ihop elena murphy,
Jiamei wu, Alissa Schapiro, Rachel Schapiro, matthew Schapiro,
Jill barber, jill biden, joe biden, james denviney, scott Jackson,
Toyal honda, k. p. Gibson,
Joseph bruff, foot & ankie, gulf south,
Wabash-washburn-harvard-servile
Sasha Obama, malia Obama, michelle robinson, barack Obama,
Tulane parking servie, ollie taylor,
Hearst zhu, jingtao hu, jingping xi, liyuan oeng, mingze xi, qi qin,
Sue nicholson, valet lemonm everst venetian, Philip noel, alan noel,
Dai yonghui, zhu taohui, zhu taozhi, dai qun e, cheng jiaqing, wang xinzhou,
Peng houping, peng yuan, shuai huazi, wang jiuzi, yang guoping, wang wuquan,
Wang Min, Guan moye, Zhang Fei, Guan Yu, Yang Suo, Yang Mo, Sun Jiguang
Yan Heyuan, Yan Yizhi, Yan anzhi, maz barry, bruce barry, curt sharp

Vladimir petror, paisley sharp, robin Sabrina ku, Loraine chan, lan yang, ken fok
Jingling wu, kim wilcox, guoping he, jiaqing cheng, xiaolan xu, aiqunn li, honglan sun
Feng huang chuanqi, shui mu nian hua, bi Fujian, cui jian, cai guoqing, dong yi

Sarah
|
|
|

Proch, shea, eunnels, chan, constantin, parish, thorrick, palin, Tulane, Loyola,
Cottrell, prtichard, Wilson, wood, fu, yan, xu, xi, peng, wang, guan, zhu, fan, yin, yan,
liu, gong, chu, shi, tu, lu, meng, zhang, dong, tian, zhen, song, mao, qian, tan, tang,
Yang, liang, wu, cai, wei, lin, li, liao, hu, hua, huang, cheng, shuai, yu, yuan, jiao, ji,
zhou, dai, feng, fei, zhao, han, hang, mi, bu, pan, luo, xia, shang, suo, zeng, guo, ni

A circle of Sarahs
All seem hard-working
Thanks to Arianna Blatt
Pontchartran Vineyard
Aly buffett
Or
Altison buffett
John Bel Edwards
Nurah Lambert

How martin yorke sees st. Tammany Fishing pier

Rainbow grocery
Croele Ice Cream shop
Peng Rongrong, Guan Li, Yang Caihong, Yang Aihong do good business
They see HER------

She has spikes
Which is soft cottons
Lisa Maddox is her manager on boating joy
Pat brister is the way to obtain advantages
Let us run after Ahoy, Matey's jack jay saux thanksgiving drive
On behalf of Donalld Villere, Mike Cooper, Freddy Drennen,
We take Jerry Brown, Ane Gust, Mark Brown, Derby Brown into our view,
Recording Jean Lafitte swamp walks
Long shadow behind
Short river snakes beyond our imaginations
Way to go,
Susan Boggs, Marissa Mayer, Zachary Bogue, Aly Buffett

Palmetto / Carrollton

CVS pharmacy, Stroelitz Eagle,
Corner Store to Exxon in Front,
The traffic light is green
All cars drive through Xavier~Loyola~Iowa~Evanston~Tulsa~Los Angeles~Tampa
technology, on Hollygrove / Forshey /Forcher /Drayros /Elysian / Palmer streets,
Dove and Peacock spread wings to fly,
Sheng comes,
Tom comes,
Amela comes,
Abbey comes,
Steadman comes,
Melinda comes,
….
The Richmond street is crowded

The New Orleans Advocate and more

Incredible human
They roam Domino pizza hut a lot
Matt Sledge and Keith Spera won't assume quiting,
Come on,
Let's dvocate Bywater nola and lily rain chicken walks,
…
Tangier and Riffi meet Ewing Clark,
Steven Jobs, Beverly Warren, Kay Baker, Zig Ziglar, all use
Warren Buffett, Joseph Butt, Carol Ayala, and John Nicklow to win,
They do obtain
Richard Allen, Heidi Nelson, and Ted Cruz's attention
Despite that Don Belt, Amy Tan, Amy Carey, and Brian Desmond Hurst
Disagree to print Loyola under anything
But itself….
A good neighbor to Larry Gosney, Jeff Bryant, and Scott Tulane

Jacquiline Keennedy

She knows
She is quiet
Gordonn Russell sets up a Vans shop,
Peter Strasser announces Chaffe McCall law firm justification,
When Mark Brown prints Gerald Clancy, Steadman Upham, Jay Nixon, and Rick Perry,
They mean to back up,
So, Jack Kennedy is remembered by David Hammer,
She is a decent soul
To Robert Siodmak, Janet Ruscher, Kim Sherman, Edward Herbert, and Aly buffett

Kay Salady's Ivan Foxwelll Yacht

She writes under Andy jin
She hears and agrees with Melania Trump,
She posts under angela zhu
She boasts Jeff Adelson voting slots
She manages Ramon Antonio Vargas.
She has Jackie Hunter in her honor roll
She rejects Michael Davidson,
She is a big fan to Jung Yan,
She reads books by Terry Rattigan, Jingle Yan,
She agrees with poet Lottie Evelyn Williams,
She pushes Alee Waugh to google engine,
She knows Robin Li, Yanhong Li, Weiping Li, Tao Li, Guan Li, Bing Li,
She airdrives Hurricane Nat, Harvey, Emma, Judy, Abbey, Amelia, Thingy
All the way

From Houston, Texas

---->
    ----->

        ------->

            Seattle, Washington

Bush City and George Trump

Mixed heads
We go forward
Get lost at Bayou hot Wings lunch party

Morgan city Abbeville, and Yanji city Jennings home

Sisters,
Abbeville and Jennings
They sit on map of Utah,
They wish to visit relative Louisiana,
They pay a news named The Times---Picaynne,
They quote "Headline " from Doug MacCash,
They trust Jeff Bezos, J. K. Rowling, Pat Mather Gordon Brown Ceton along,
Greetings to Mark Berman, Rann Wang, Taryn Brown, Delvin Barrett,
They, secretly protect Kimberly Middle East,
Ignoring Melisa Mills, Barbara Boyd, Troy Henry, and Sam Clancy,
They dream about being known,
Been driven,
Been pushed,
Been spoiled,
Been educated,
And been sought

Thanks to Bruno Wu, Lan Yang, Jianfeng Gu, Leo Ku,
Sabrina Robin Ku, Loraine Chan, Tom l. Wu, Phillipe Guan

Starwood above Joel Sligman, Delores Conway, and Alan Yu

According to Hu Jintao and Liu Yongqing,
Today's voice is about democracy and freedom of ordinary folks,
Which makes Donald Trump, Barack Obama, George Bush, and Bill Clinton thrilled

Clouds gather
All the way from Mars
Passing Jupiter
Spiritual Jesus and Mary join Joseph, Matthew, John, Christina, Emily, and Abbey

Al Gore and Tipper Gore know their fame,
James Gunn, Kazuo Yamazaki, Nidna Yamazaki, and Zhao Wei forgive others,
Tang Kun, Tang Jingqiu, Dai Wangbing, Zhou Tong, Yan Ji, Tu Jun, and Hu Huijiao
vote

Andrea Seligman,
Peter Seligman,
Kevin Murphy,
David Falcon,

Eric Wood, Stephan Wilson, Ari Wood, George Wilson, Michael Fitts, Burns Hargis,
All seem okay with Suri Cruise, Katie Holmes, Shiloh Pitt-Jolie, Brad and Angela Pitt
If I agree to let Lee Fan and Yao Peng enjoy Atlanta, Georgia,
Bessy Fan, Charles Fan, Jiuxiang Fan, Songzi Hu, Qiao Hu, Lingling Hu, Qun E Yang,

Etc. Seem cheerful
And helpful
Under Bingyu Yu, Daihong Zhu, Wenhui Wu, Hongwen Kong, Barron Trump, James Park, Gloria ann Page, Victor Carl Page, Steven Garmin, Henry Zarrow, H. A, Chapman

Lower School ~~~Vendome Johnson

Arrowhead Newman
A. B. Freeman
    Elena murphy
    Samantha murphy
    Sheng Wu
    Wenjia Xu
    Cynthia Francisco
    Emily Quinn
    Mingming (Kayla) Zhang
    Kong Yuan
    Sofina Yuan
    Ivan Dai
    Sifang Zhang
    Hannah Xie
    Yu Dou
    Tianjian Wu
    Jing Wu
    Diane Li
    Oliver Li
    …

    folks fly here
    they tell us about joseph Octavia
    or Nashville Loyola
    I read a note from Kay Ryan,
    It says Isidore Newman School. 1903
    Doris Stone office,
    David Oreck Class,
    James Park Fitbit,

Audubon Park,

Audubon Zoo,
Percival Stern Lech
Claiborne Boggs library
Milton Latter Levy student center

A few fame lit a star bright
Nightly sky glows
Unexpected crashes
Steamboats bump melody to passegers at New Orleans downtown shore

Sanlin
Marx
Alex
Paisley

Sarah and john run marathon on Laura Ingalls Wilder stories,
Cute childhood
George Houston Odgen and Hannah Audubon follow twitter
They put Dou Zhenjie, Yang Jianlin, Li Jingna, Chao Hui, He Yan, and Liu Hua on
Facebook

Joseph Lopinto, Ian McGee, Danny Clyde, and Jammy King

All three dragonflies sit on an Mobile fuel,
Printing their handprints in Heaven,
Knowing the foureyed frogs
And who gives pro-cut a thumb up,
They stay calm, croaking November air in Merry Christmas mod

It doesnot matter
Who is a neighborly friend to Sarah Parish,
If Jefferson Parish library adopts many children,
Susan and Steven, Libby and Claibourne, Kathryn and William,
John and Janet, Linda and Allan, Igor and Julie, Amelia and Steven,
All may feel relaxed

Qwik chek, terry jones, Cheryl mainor, Charles page,
Benji wojin, chlooe wojin, sophie Schmidt, Alison Schmidt,
Allex page, james page, larry page, Lucinda southworth,
A google bird could represent a crow-crab fish as their favorites

Forget about Angie Ben's assumptions
Felicia Smith and Jerry Funk can do well

Burger King, Glenn Jones, Dart Vincennes

A unique thing
Created by Metairie Hargis
Dennis Hanwell sings Lyrics
Janice Brown places a CD on the Hampton Inn breakfast

Iresisable
Absolutely interesting
A good company to clarion herald
Neighborly friends

Silent auctions
Poetry speaks 401 316 8960
We do love Amelia Wilson, san Francisco, and melyssa allen

www.ingramcontent.com/pod-product-compliance
Lightning Source LLC
Chambersburg PA
CBHW031904170626
46807CB00004B/1889